Crayola®
TIP'S TRAVEL
PUZZLE PAD
™

a note to parents

This puzzle travel pad is full of varied, fun activities for children who are starting to learn about numbers and counting.

Let your child work through the book at his or her own pace and be prepared to give help when it is needed.
You may like to sit together and talk about each of the different activities.

Crayola Crayons, Colouring Pens and Pencils are ideal to use with this pad.

1 one

Colour one sandcastle.

Draw one flag in the sandcastle.

Colour one bucket.

2 two

Colour two teddy bears.

2 two

Colour two teddy bears.

Draw a balloon for each teddy bear.

Colour two trains and two balls.

3 three

Colour three people.

3 three

Colour three cars and three people.
Draw three trees.

1 one   2 two   3 three

Colour one tractor.

Colour two dogs.

Colour three chickens.

4 four

Colour four bees.

4 four

Colour four petals on each flower.
How many flowers?
Draw a bee on each flower.

5 five

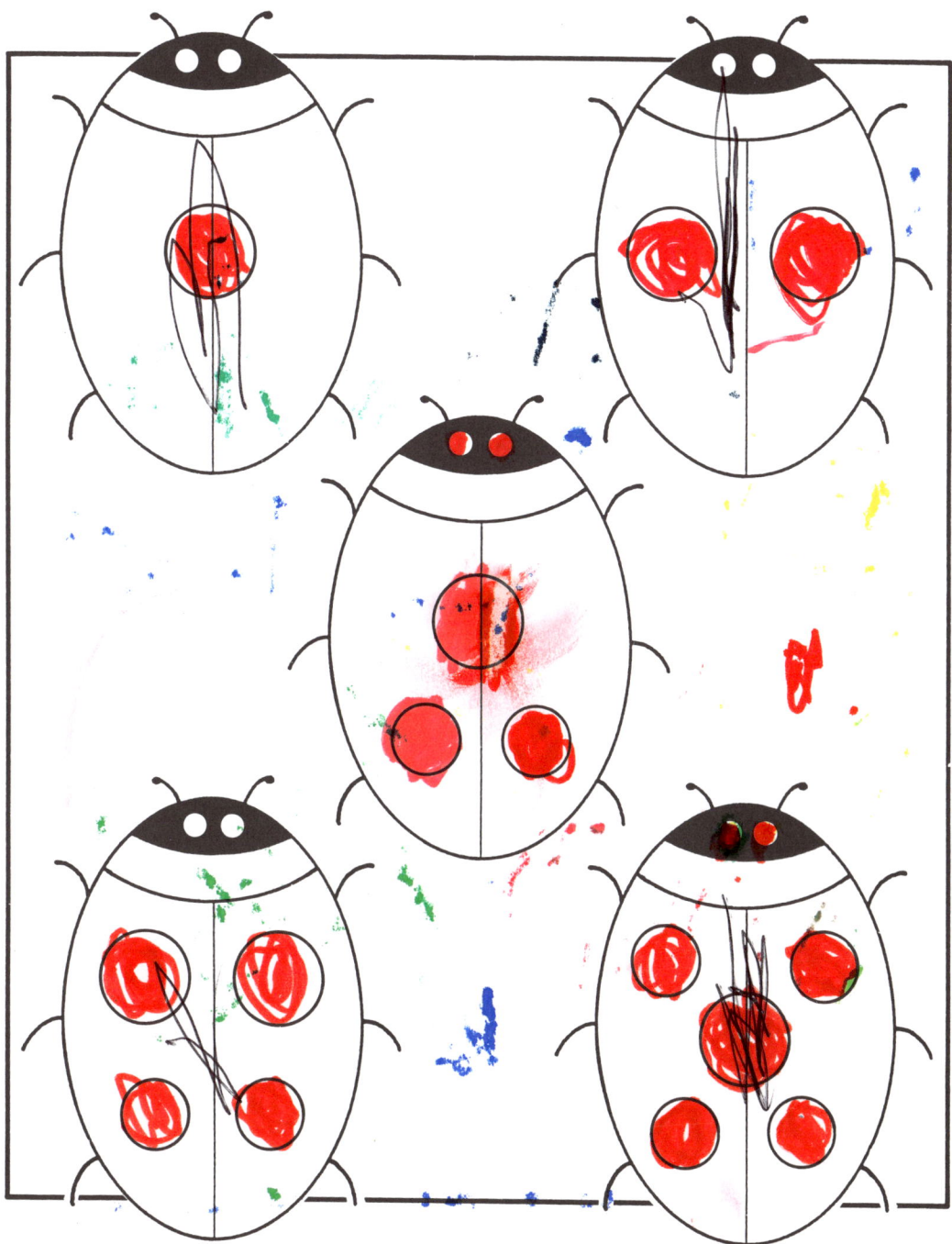

Colour five ladybirds.

5 five

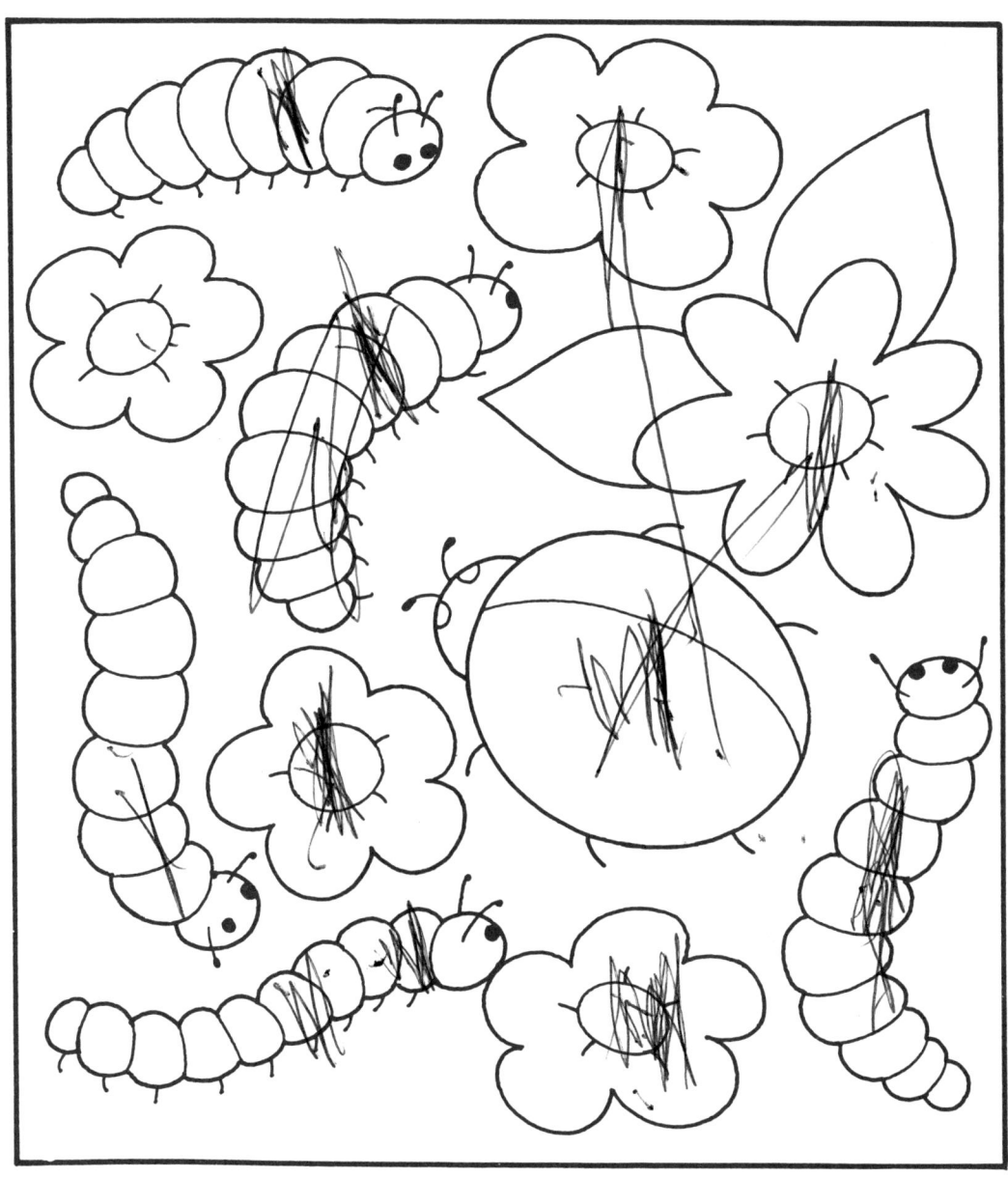

Colour five flowers and five caterpillars.
Draw five spots on the ladybird.

2 3 4 5

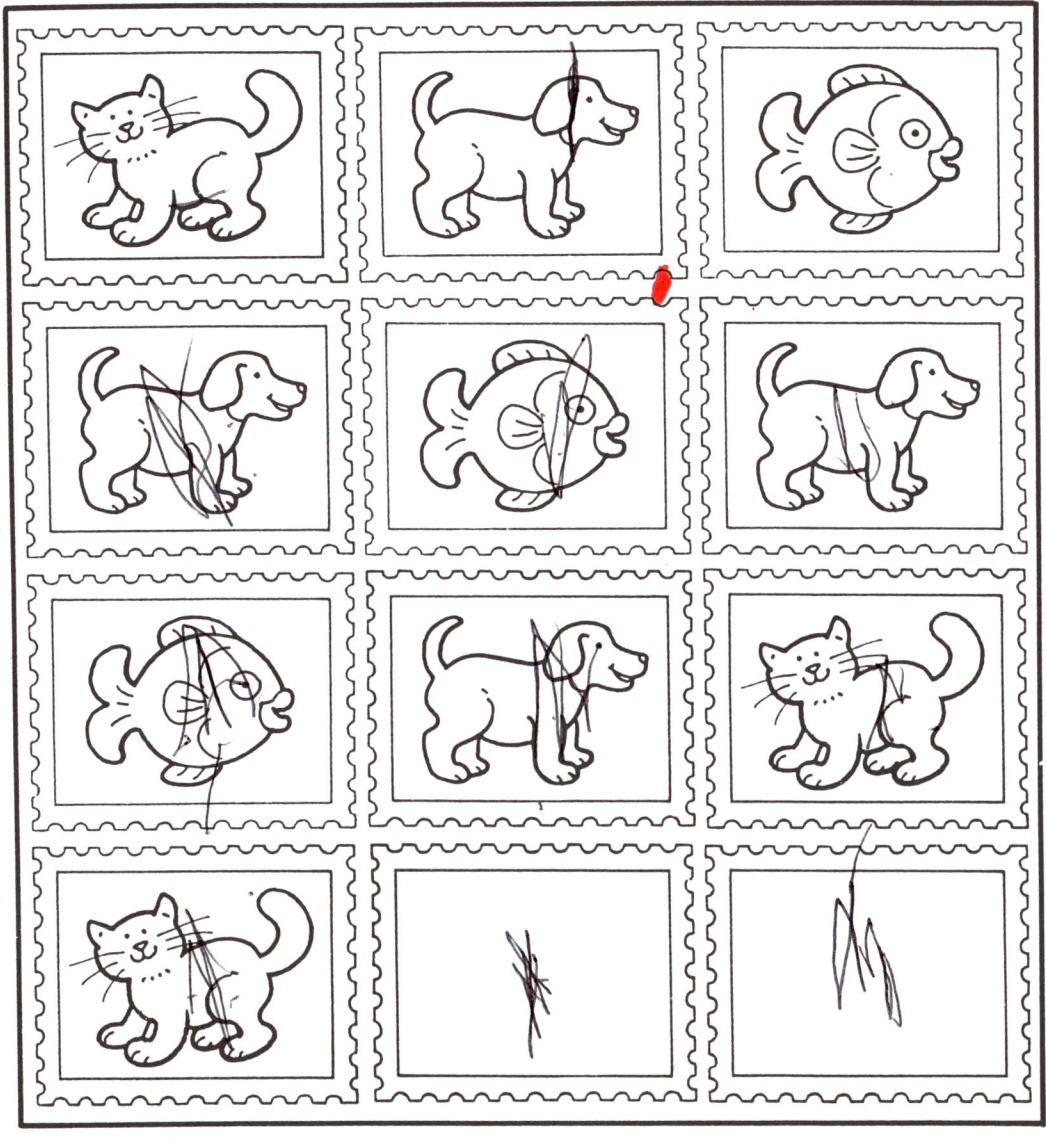

Colour three cat stamps.

Colour four dog stamps.

Draw two more fish stamps.

1 2 3 4 5

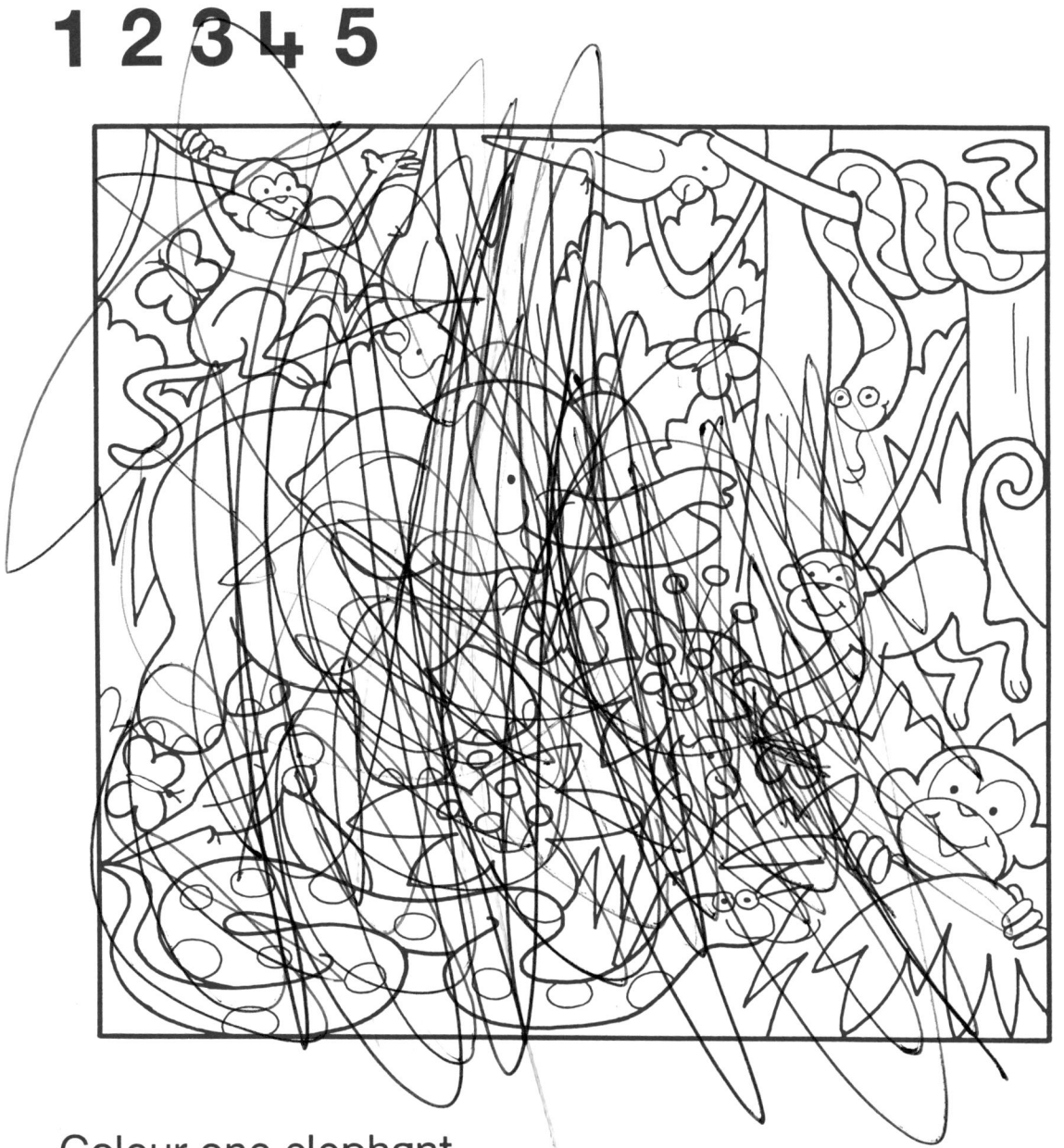

Colour one elephant.

Colour two snakes.

Colour three monkeys.

How many parrots can you find?

How many butterflies?

1 2 3 4 5

Colour two birds.

Colour three frogs.

Colour four fish.

How many lilypads can you see?

How many ducks?

1 2 3 4 5

Join each dog to its kennel.
Match the number to the spots.

1 2 3 4 5

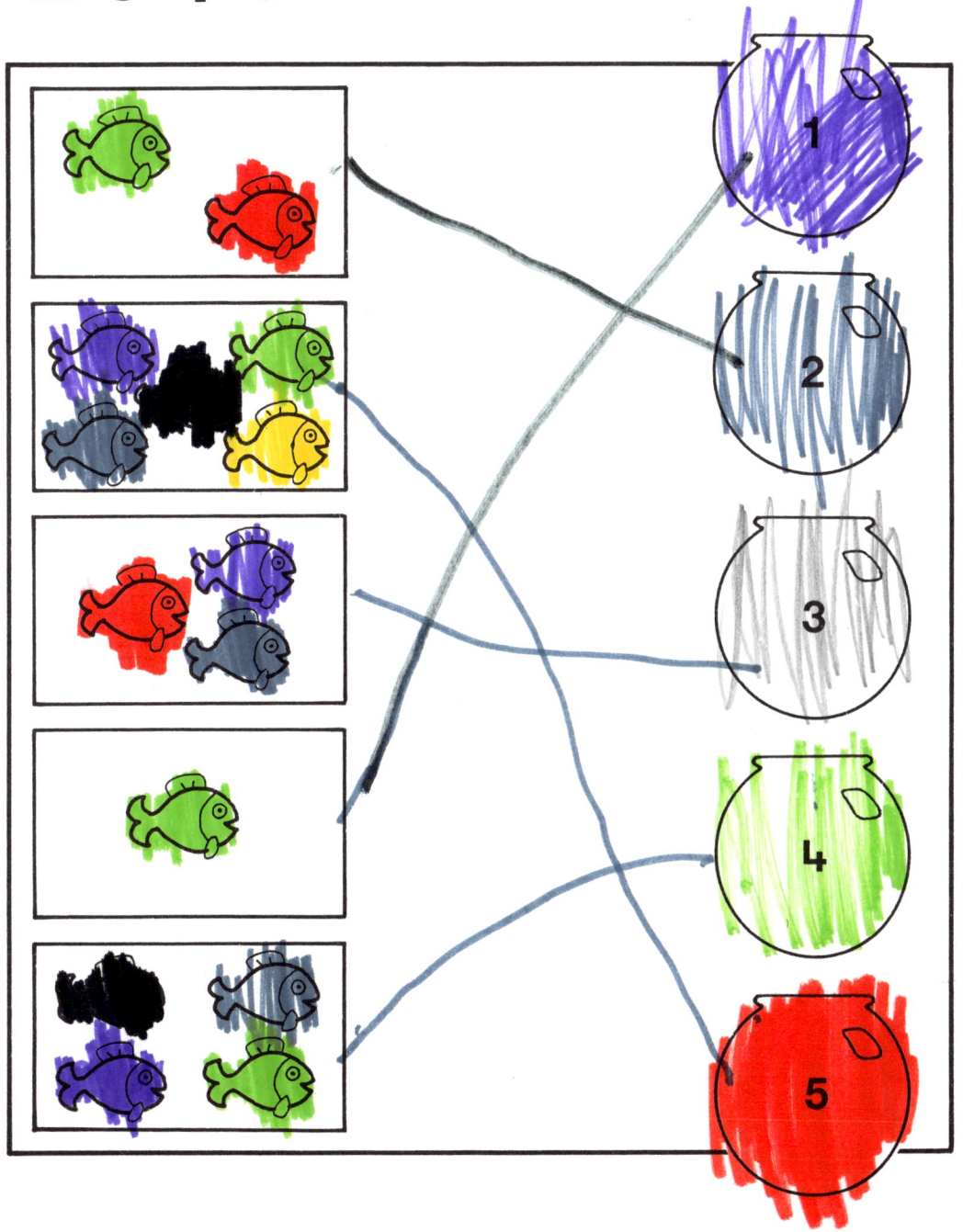

Join each set of fish to its bowl.
Match the number to the fish.

5 dots

Who is driving the car?
Join the dots in the right order.

5 dots

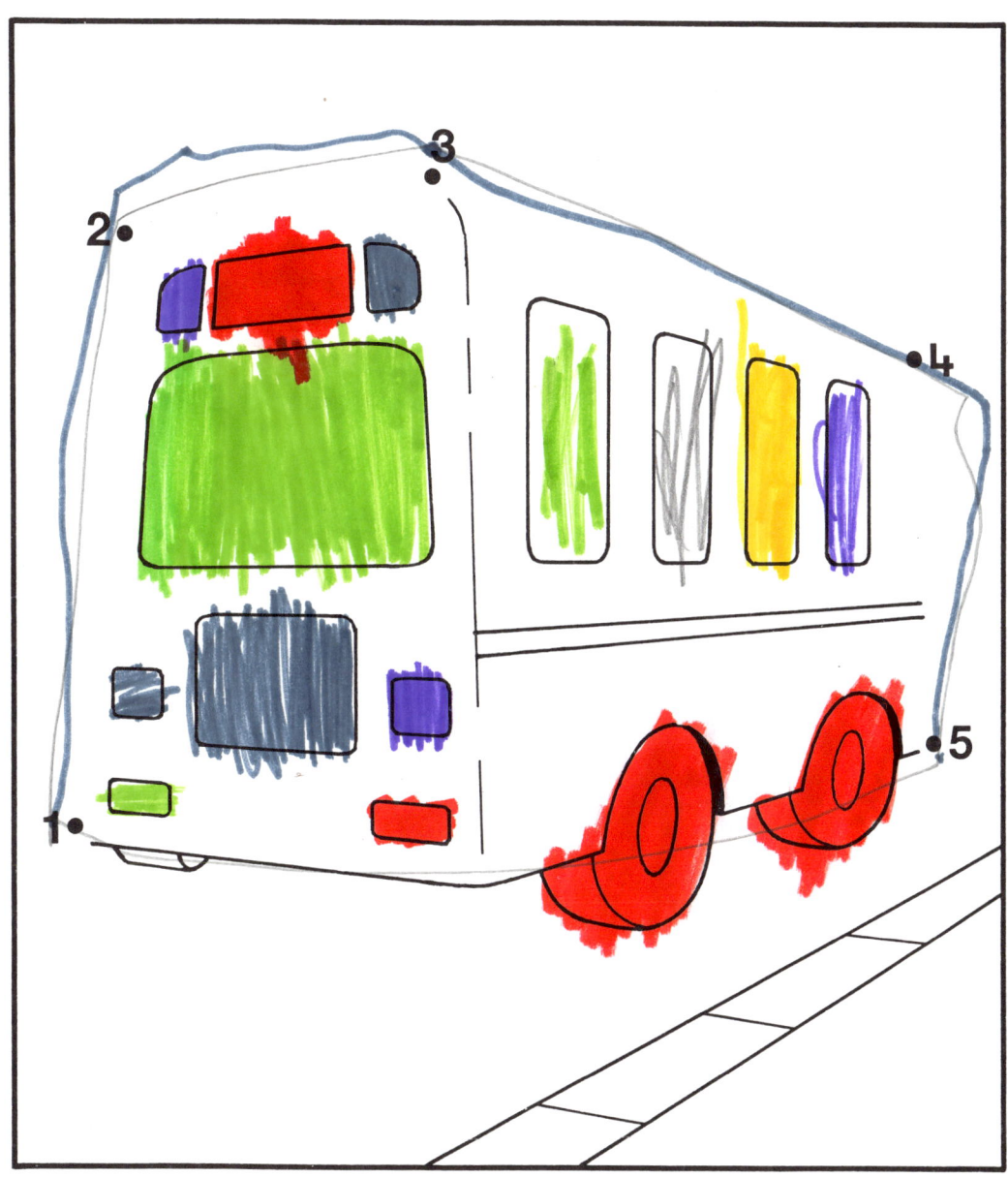

What is coming along the road?
Join the dots in the right order.

6 six

Colour six buttons.

6 six

Colour six buckets.

Draw a hat on each clown's head.

Colour six clowns.

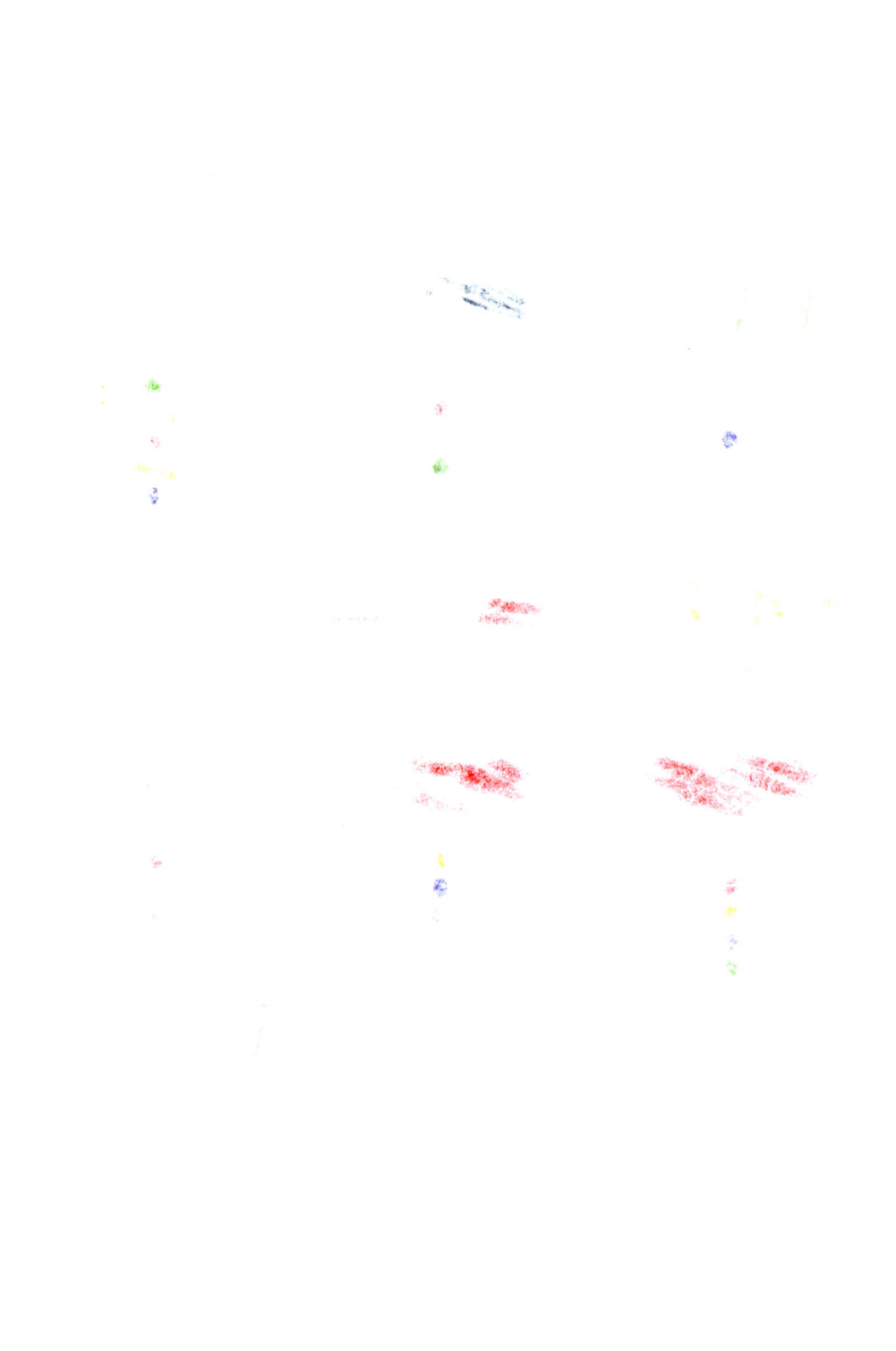

7 seven

Colour seven houses and seven stars.

7 seven

Colour seven owls.

Draw seven stars in the sky.

8 eight

Colour eight starfish and eight shells.

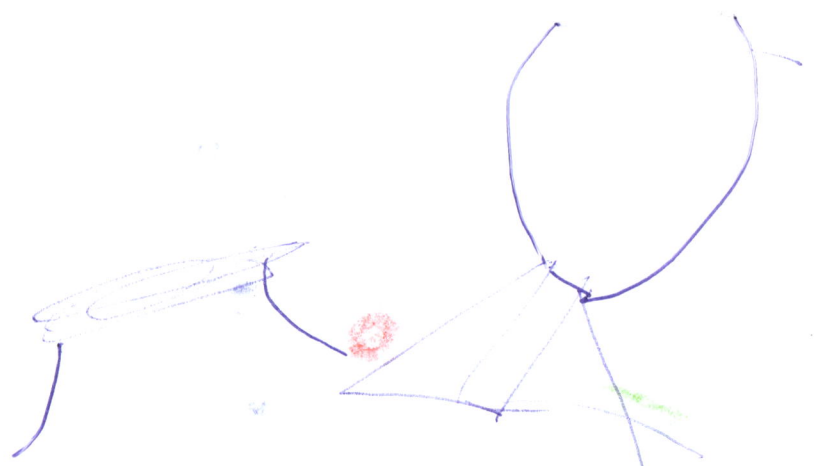

6 six 7 seven 8 eight

How many aliens can you see?
How many rockets?
Draw two more craters.

6 six 7 seven 8 eight

How many bricks are in each tower?
Draw your own tower of bricks.
How many bricks does it have?

9 nine

Colour nine candles.

9 nine

Colour nine hats.

Draw a cherry on each cake.

10 ten

Colour ten presents.

Draw ten balls on the tree.

How many stars can you see?

8 eight 9 nine 10 ten

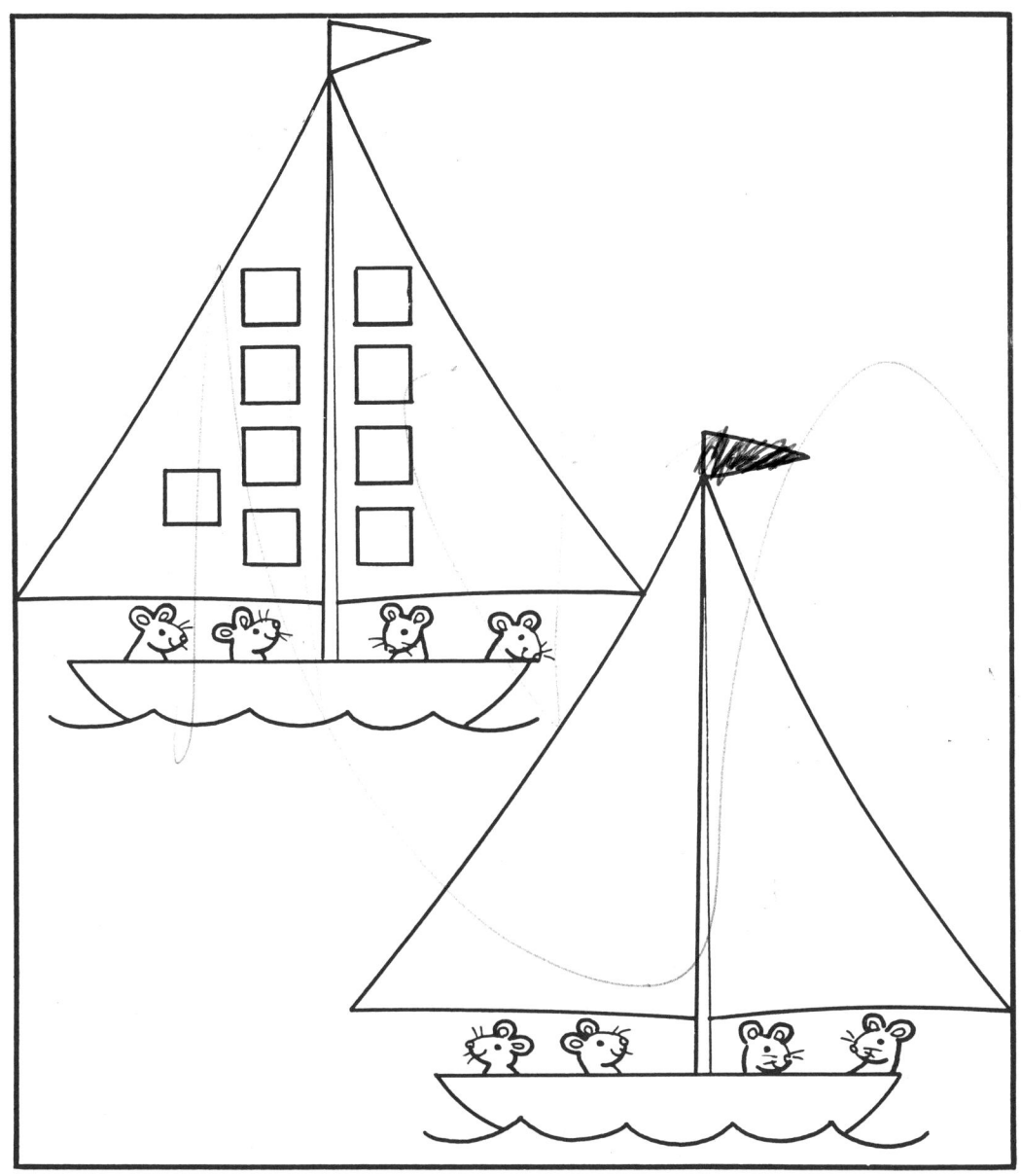

How many squares are on the sail?
Draw ten squares on the other sail.

8 eight 9 nine 10 ten

How many apples are on the tree?

How many on the ground?

Colour the rungs on the ladders.

How many apples in the basket?

Draw ten apples on the other tree.

All at Sea

Try to find 10 sea words in the wordsearch.

These are the words to look for.

☑ anchor ☐ flag ☑ funnel ☑ lifeboat ☑ mast
☑ porthole ☑ rope ☑ sailor ☑ seagull ☑ waves

a	n	c	h	o	r	k	y	l	l
i	q	a	s	g	o	t	r	s	a
t	s	u	a	n	p	z	c	e	j
w	e	l	i	f	e	b	o	a	t
e	f	t	l	s	g	k	n	g	l
r	u	w	o	m	a	s	t	u	a
e	n	s	r	h	n	l	x	l	g
d	n	p	o	r	t	h	o	l	e
o	e	t	h	h	r	e	n	e	i
n	l	e	u	o	w	a	v	e	s

6 7 8 9 10

6	
7	
8	
9	
10	

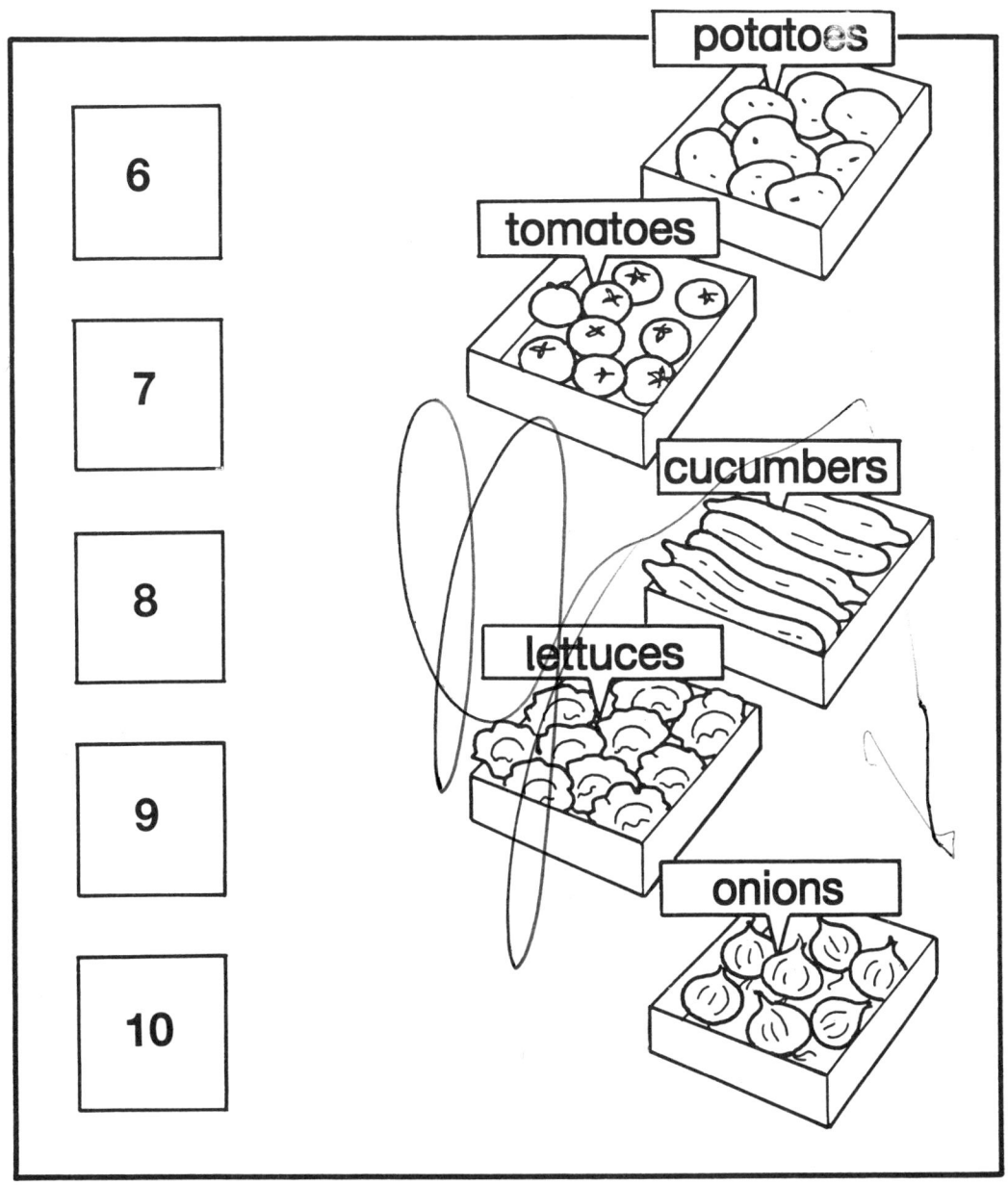

potatoes

tomatoes

cucumbers

lettuces

onions

How many of each vegetable can you see?
Join each one to its number.

6 7 8 9 10

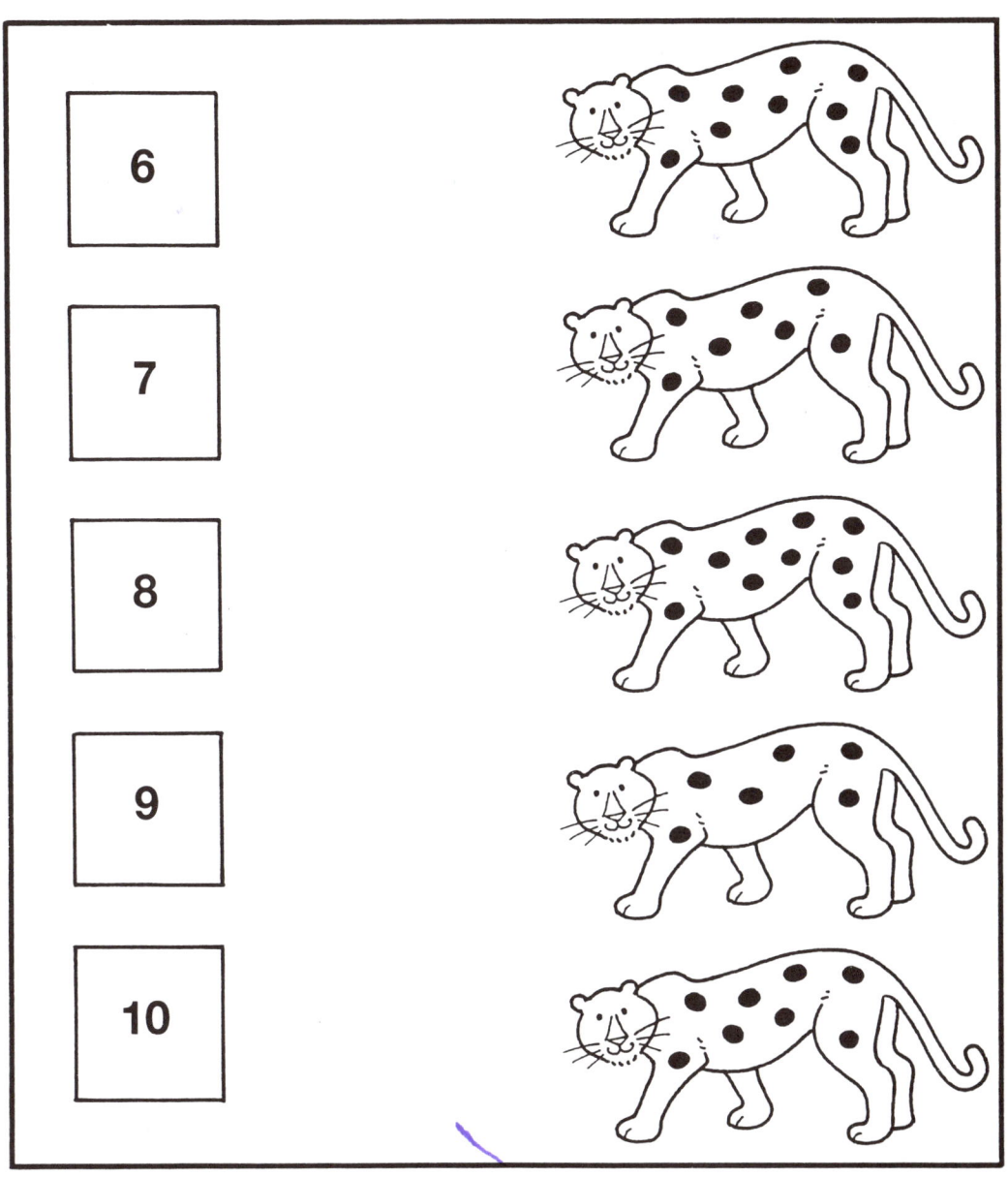

6	
7	
8	
9	
10	

How many spots on each leopard?
Join each one to its number.

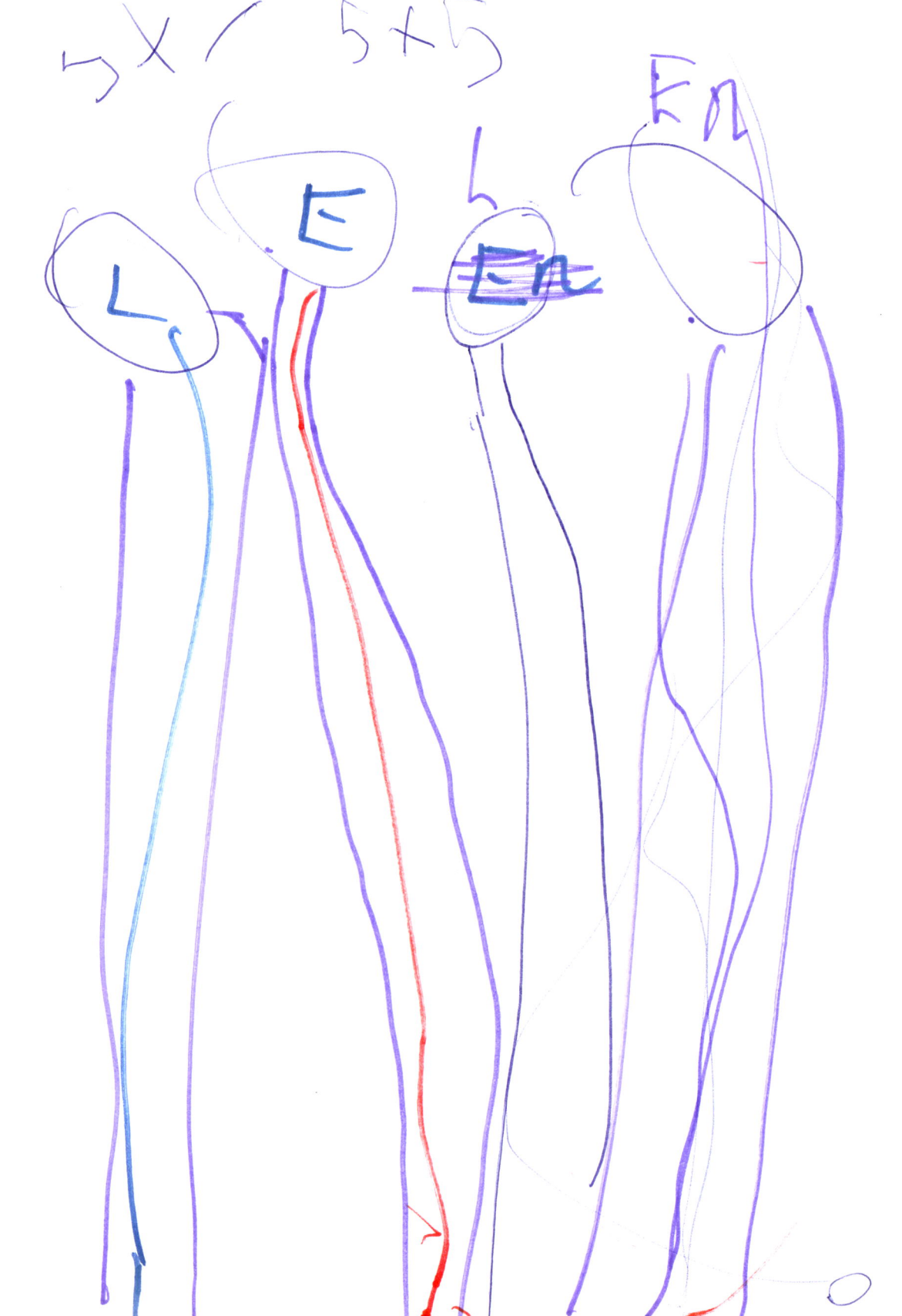

1 2 3 4 5 6 7 8 9 10

How many windows in each house?
How many trees can you see?
How many birds? Draw two more.

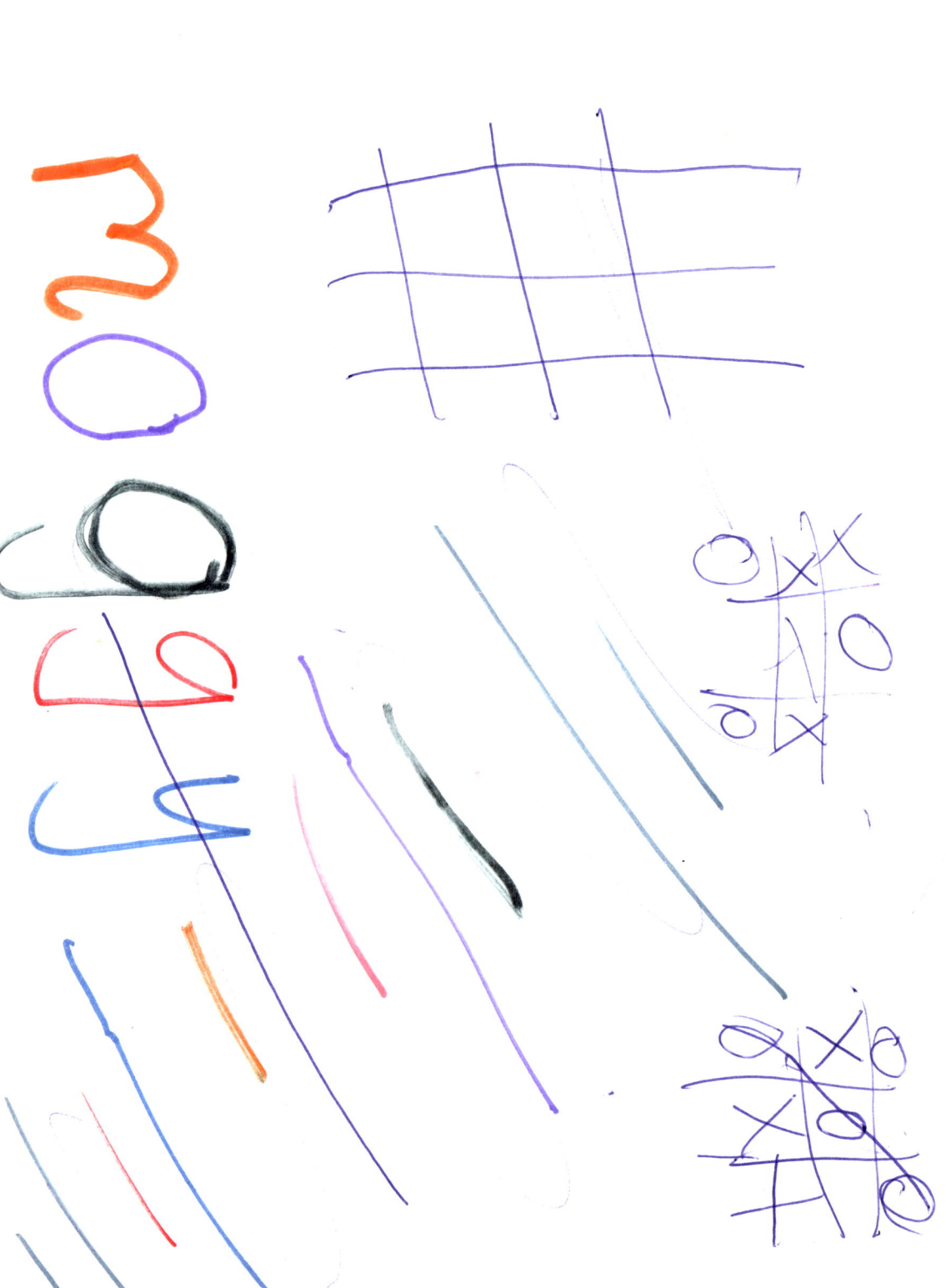

1 2 3 4 5 6 7 8 9 10

How many of each toy can you find?

Weather Words

Try to find 10 weather words in the wordsearch.

These are the words to look for.

☑ cloud ☑ fog ☑ ice ☑ lightning ☑ rain
☑ snow ☑ storm ☑ sun ☑ thunder ☑ wind

10 dots

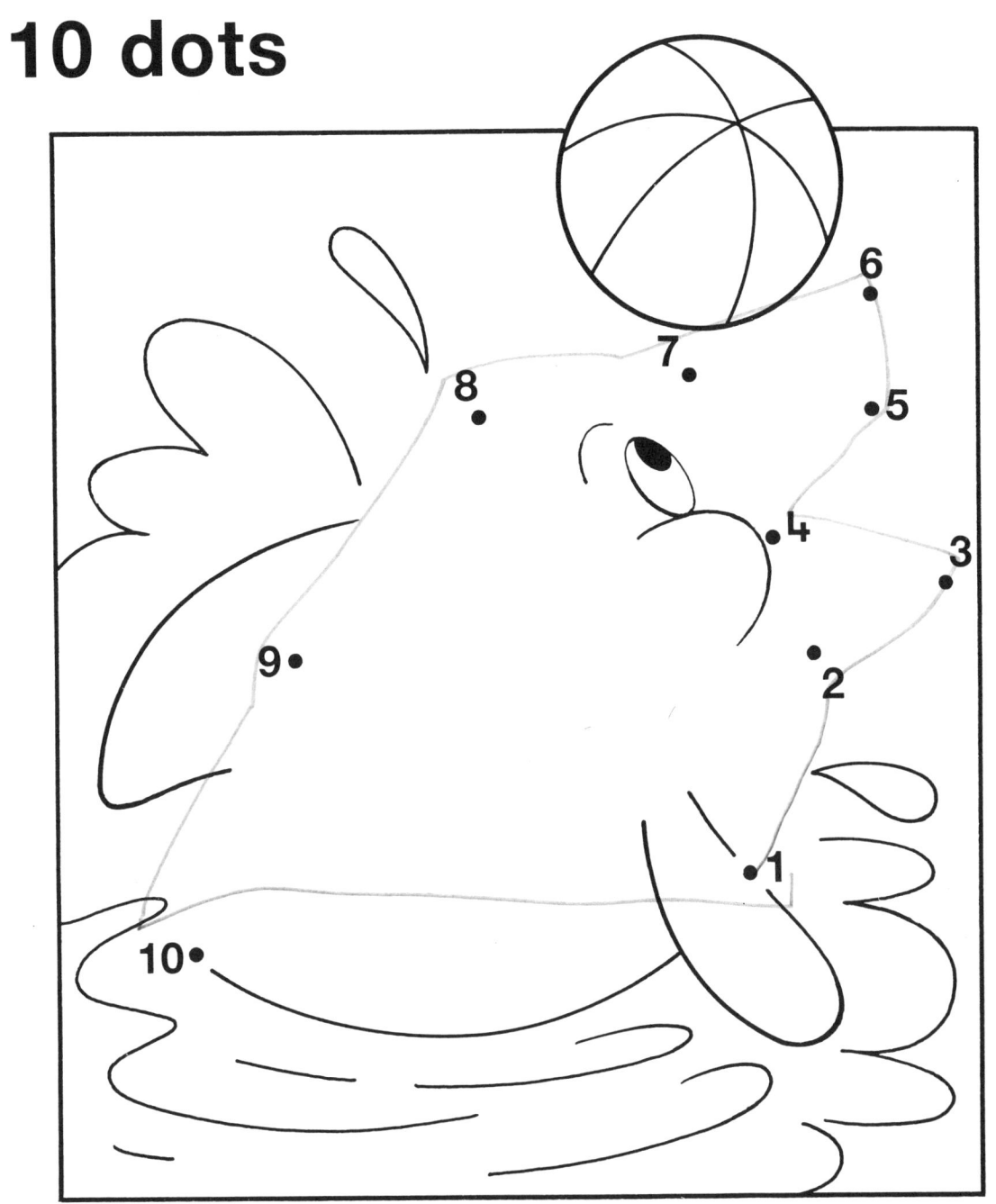

Who is playing with the ball?
Join the dots from 1 to 10 to find out.

1 to 10

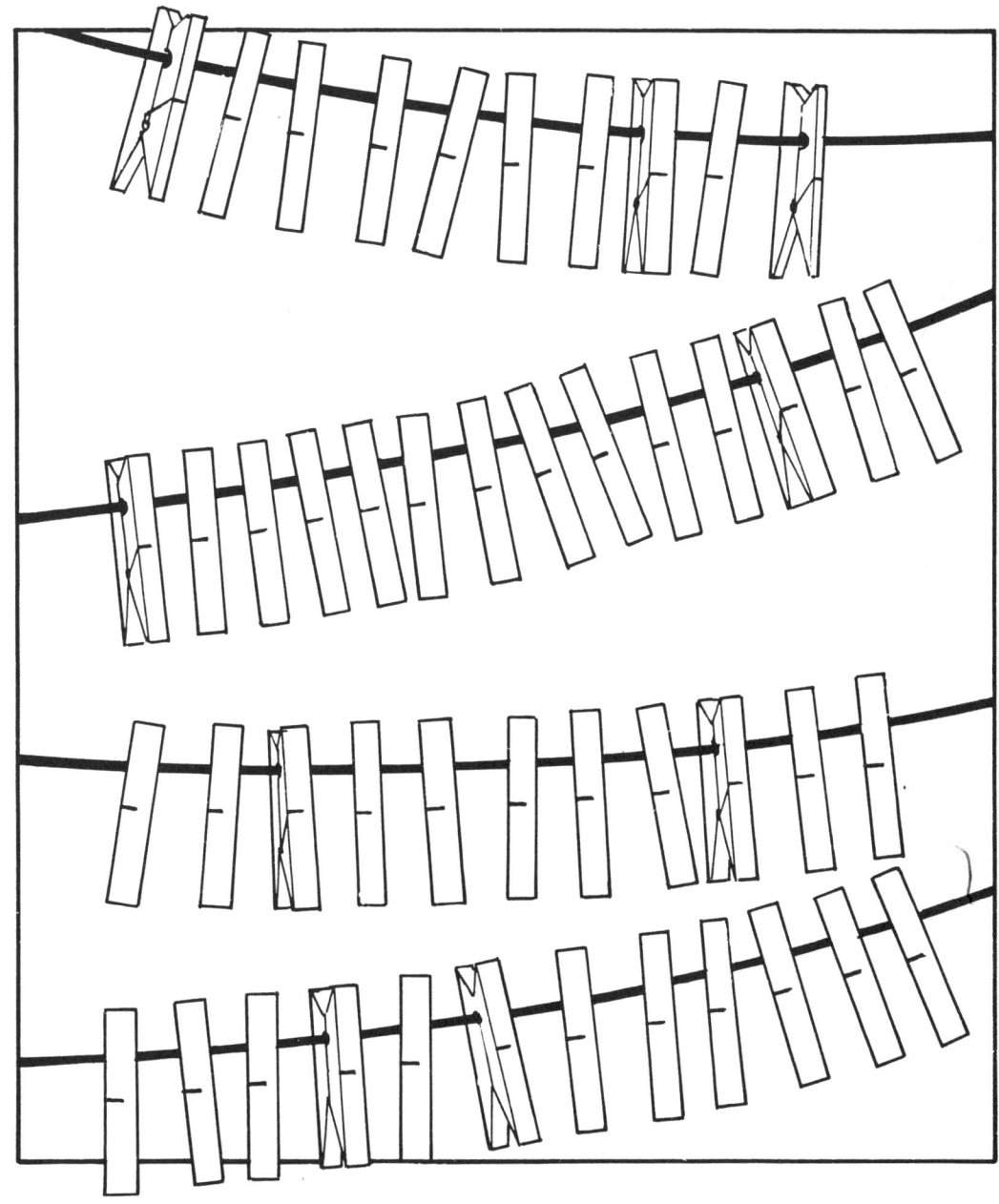

Colour ten pegs on each line.

How many pegs on each line are not coloured?

How many spots?

Play the spotty game.

Throw a dice.

Colour the spots to match the dice.

Now throw again until you have coloured all the dice.

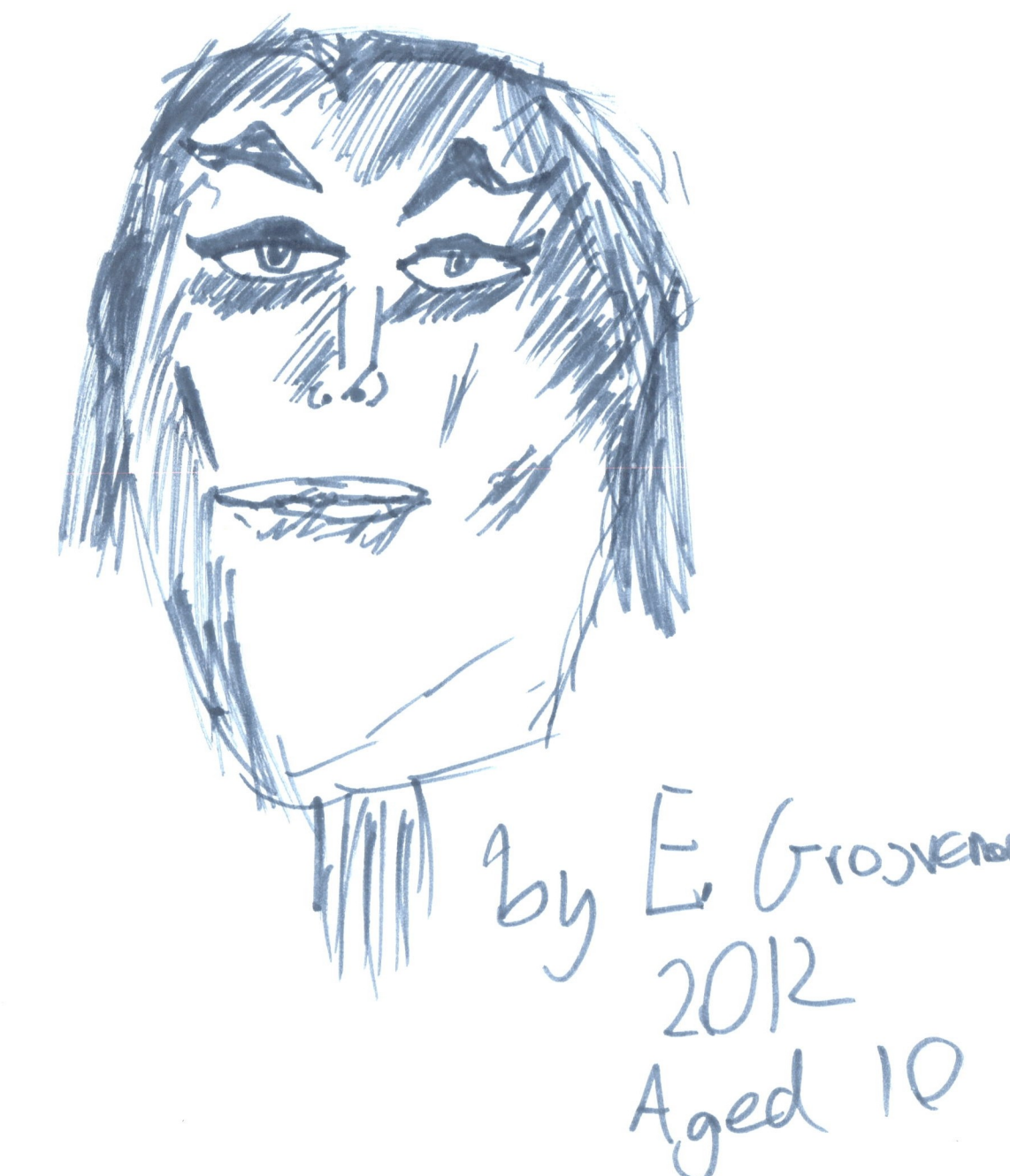

By E. Grosvenor
2012
Aged 10

Fruit Find

Try to find the names of 10 fruits in the wordsearch.

These are the words to look for.

☑ apple ☑ banana ☑ cherry ☑ grape ☑ lemon
☑ lime ☑ melon ☑ orange ☑ pear ☑ plum

a	p	p	l	e	n	w	o	e	r
i	e	s	t	w	h	i	m	t	n
o	a	f	w	u	q	i	s	c	t
g	r	a	p	e	l	b	r	h	a
i	n	t	l	k	b	h	y	e	p
m	a	o	u	l	a	z	g	r	l
e	l	e	m	o	n	n	a	r	o
l	k	t	a	d	a	j	h	y	k
o	c	e	l	r	n	e	k	l	s
n	j	s	o	p	a	q	u	p	t

1 to 10

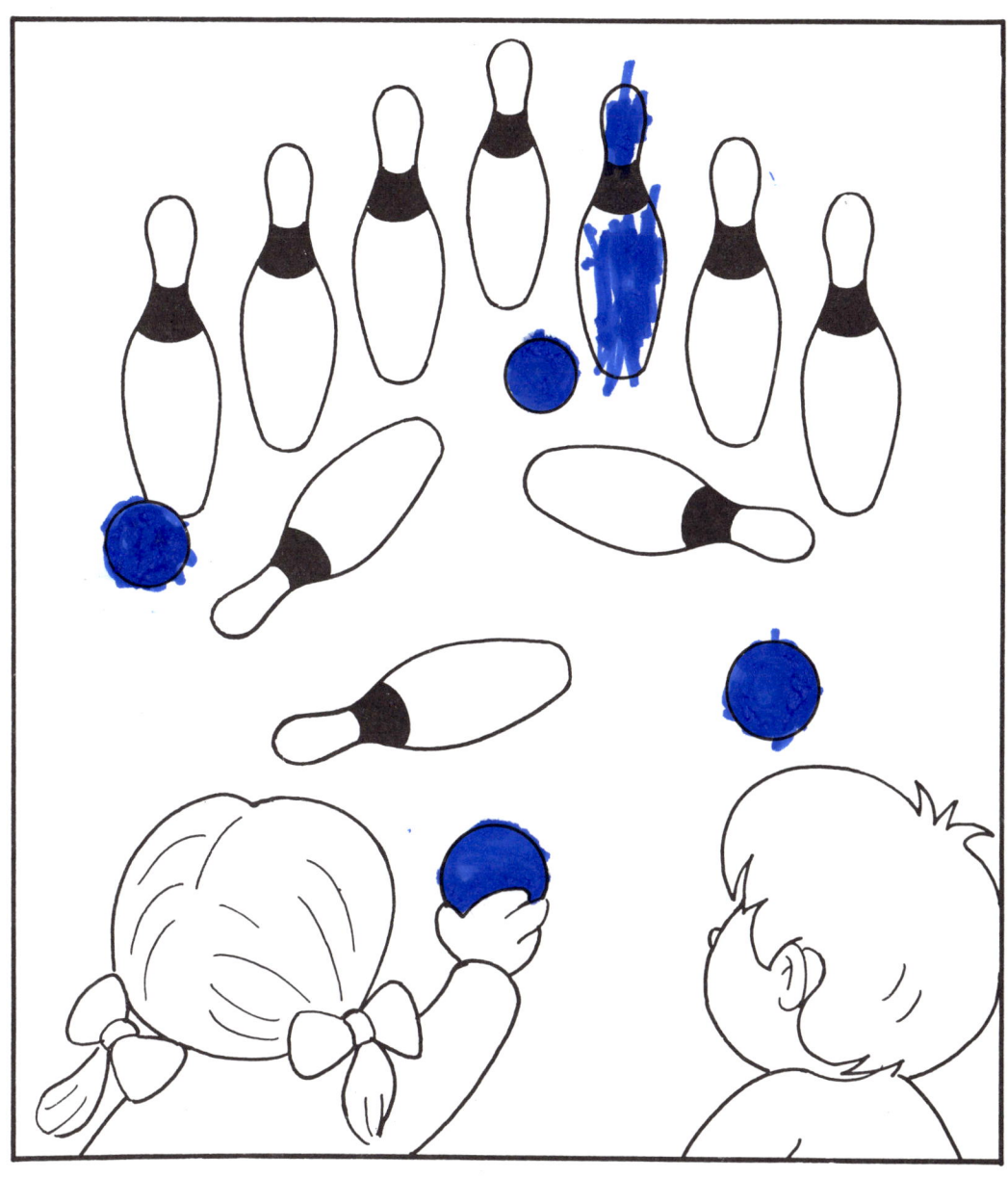

How many skittles are standing? 7

How many have fallen? 3

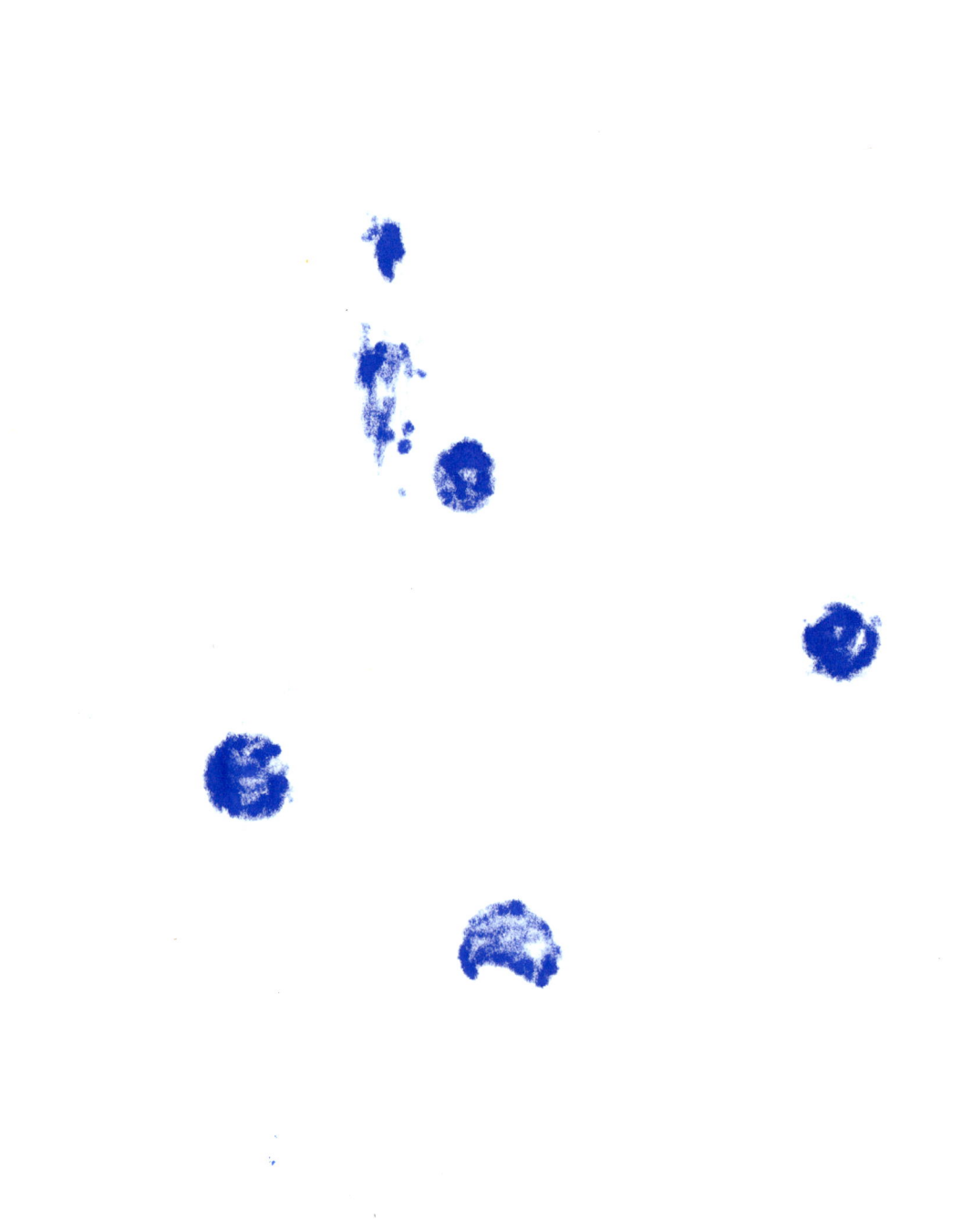

How many spots?

Draw spots on each clown's costume to match the number on the tie.

ANSWERS TO WORDSEARCHES

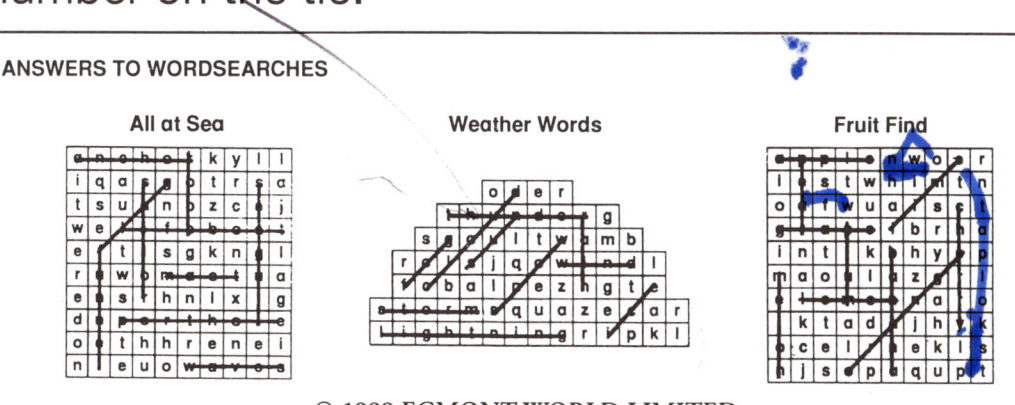

All at Sea

Weather Words

Fruit Find